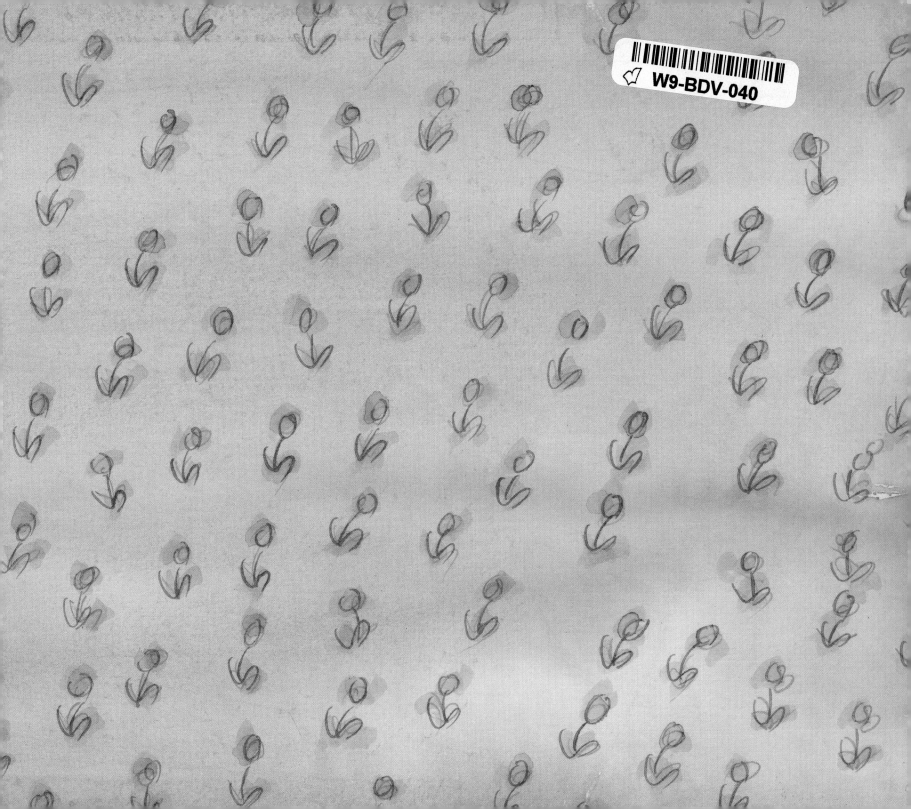

For my friend Rachel Oscar. Love, Amy

For Anne Moore. Christine

Text copyright © 2000 by Amy Hest
Illustrations copyright © 2000 by Christine Davenier

First edition 2000

Library of Congress Cataloging-in-Publication Data

Hest, Amy.
Mabel dancing / Amy Hest ; illustrated by Christine Davenier.
—1st ed.   p.   cm.
Summary: Mabel doesn't want to go to sleep while
Mama and Papa are having a dance party downstairs.
ISBN 0-7636-0746-0
[1. Bedtime—Fiction. 2. Dance—Fiction. 3. Parties—Fiction.]
I. Davenier, Christine, ill. II. Title.
PZ7.H4375Mad   2000
[E]—dc21   99-34807

2 4 6 8 10 9 7 5 3 1

Printed in Hong Kong

This book was typeset in Colwell Italic.
The illustrations were done in watercolor and ink.

Candlewick Press
2067 Massachusetts Avenue
Cambridge, Massachusetts 02140

Mabel Dancing

Amy Hest

illustrated by

Christine Davenier

CANDLEWICK PRESS
CAMBRIDGE, MASSACHUSETTS

*O*n the night of the dancing party, Mabel

blew bubbles in the bath while Mama dressed up

and Papa tied his dancing shoes. Mama blew kisses,

and Papa did, too, singing that song for Mabel.

"Shall we dance . . .

shall we dance . . .

shall we dance?"

When the bubbles were gone, Mabel wrapped herself in towels. Then she buttoned Mama's robe and it draped to the floor in bunches. She put her feet in Papa's velvet slippers that were green and she put her nose to the mirror.

"I can dance," Mabel said, and Curly Dog barked.

On the night of the dancing party,

Mabel was put to bed before the guests arrived,

and Mama tucked her in while Papa closed the

curtains. Then Papa tucked her in, and the

curtain blew and Mama's gown did, too.

"Sleep tight," they said.

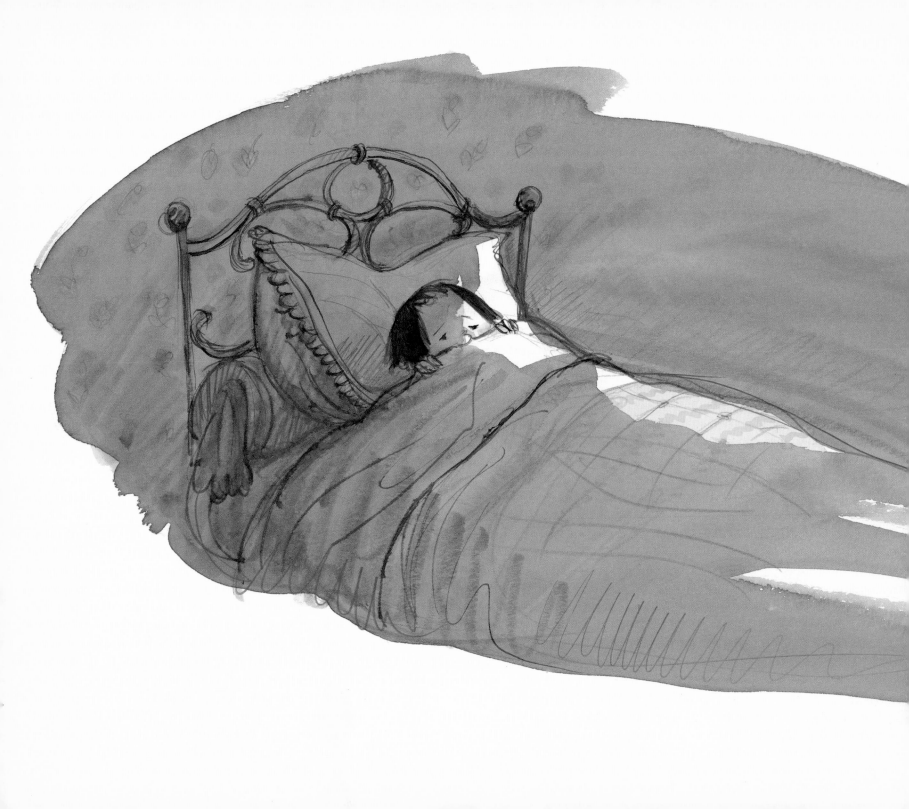

And there was Mabel, alone in the night.

From way down the stairs there was

music in the night and the music

had a way of floating up the stairs

— one, two, three —

— one, two, three —

up and up the stairs.

Mabel hopped off the bed, hopping barefoot
to the window. Curly Dog came, too, and
they stood at the glass, admiring the stars.
They counted Mabel's toes,
and there were ten.

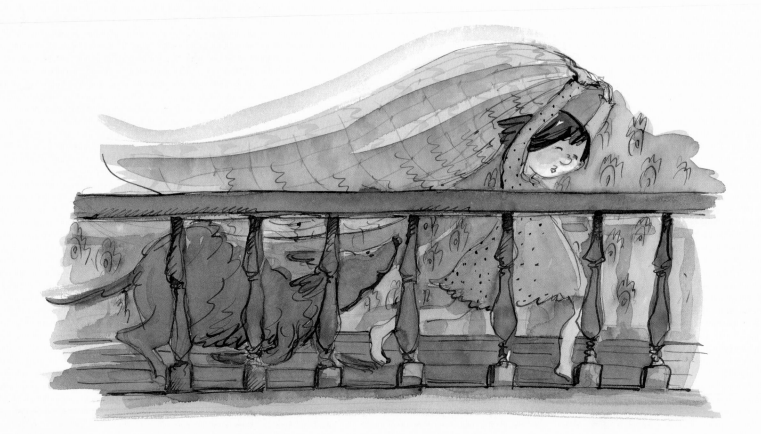

Mabel slid barefoot to the top of the stairs.

Curly Dog came, too.

They sat down
and lay down
on Mabel's
yellow blanket.

From way down the stairs there was music

in the night, and papas in bow ties. Mamas,

too, in swirling gowns, and the swirling

had a way of swooshing up the stairs

⌒ swirl, two, three ⌒

⌒ swoosh, two, three ⌒

up and up the stairs.

"You dance," Mabel said.

Curly Dog yawned instead,

thumping his tail on the blanket.

Then Mabel stood up.

"Watch me!" she said, and off she went

⌐ one, two, three ⌐

⌐ one, two, three ⌐

dancing down the stairs,

and she didn't make a sound

⌐ shhh, two, three ⌐

⌐ shhh, two, three ⌐

down and down the stairs.

Mabel twirled and jumped in the bright
party light, and her blanket blew up
like a yellow cape in the wind
making swirls.

And Mabel had a way of

spinning past the guests

~ spin, two, three ~

— spin, two, three —

floating through the rooms.

Mama and Papa loved the show, and so did
the guests. Mabel bowed in her red nightgown.

"Shall we dance?" Papa said,

and they all danced away

in the velvet light.

Mama's gown swooshed and Papa's bow tie

tickled and they danced up the stairs

⁓ one, two, three ⁓

⁓ one, two, three ⁓

up and up the stairs with Mabel blowing kisses.

On the night of the dancing party, Mabel

snuggled way down deep in the big blue bed.

Curly Dog snuggled, too. Mabel closed her eyes,

and the curtain blew like a yellow cape in the wind

making soft yellow swirls.

And from way down the stairs . . .

the music played on.

~ one, two, three ~

~ one, two, three ~

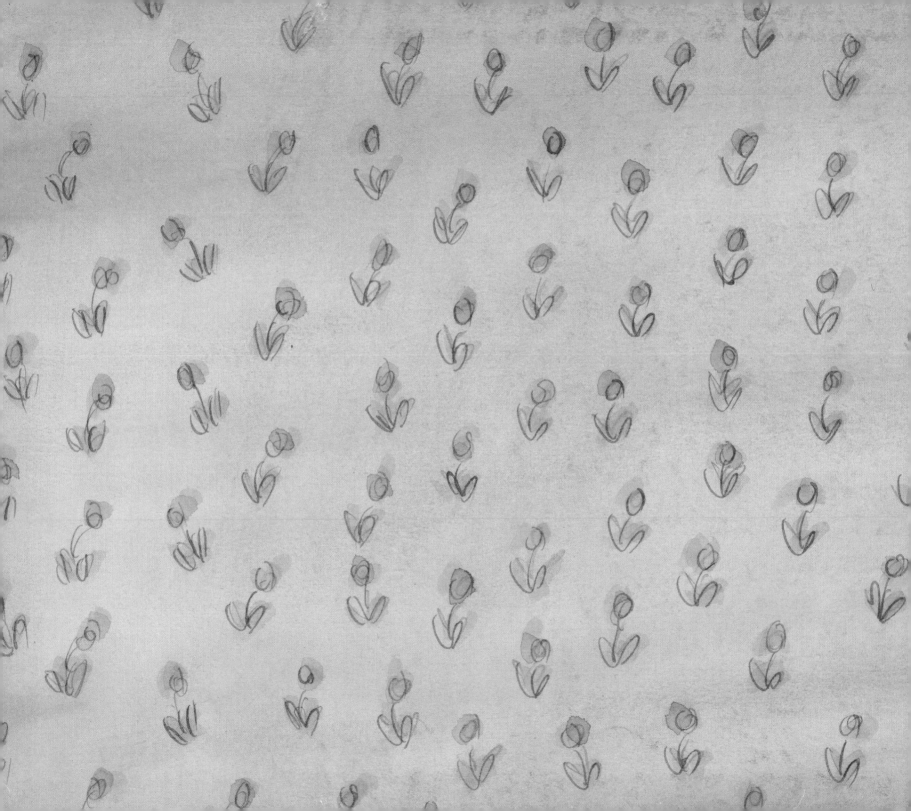